Nalani Denn. S-Wave

NAT ENOUGH

MARIA SCRIVAN

For you, reader.
You are more than enough.

Library of Congress Control Number: 2019936057

ISBN 978-1-338-53821-2 (hardcover)
ISBN 978-1-338-53819-9 (paperback)

10 9 8 7 6 5 4 3 2 1 20 21 22 23 24

Printed in China 62
First edition, April 2020
Edited by Megan Peace
Book design by Phil Falco
Publisher: David Saylor

CONTENTS

All About Me! 1

Magazine Girl 11

Hurdles and Other Obstacles 21

Snoozefest 29

Raining Cats and Frogs 47

Hats Off 77

Cupid Strikes Again 89

Dance (But Everyone Is Watching) 99

Sing like No One Can Hear You 107

Costumes, Please 117

Showstopper 125

Smoke and Mirrors 147

A Day in the Life 157

About Time 163

What's the Story? 177

What's for Lunch? 191

The Envelope, Please 197

Stand Up 211

A Day in the Life of a Frog If She Wasn't Made out of Jell-O 223

ALL ABOUT ME!

HI! I'M NATALIE.

(AND THIS IS MY SKETCHBOOK.)

I LOVE TO WRITE AND DRAW.

I ALSO LOVE TO PLAY WITH MY CAT AND DOG,

RIDE MY BIKE,

AND HANG OUT WITH MY BEST FRIEND, LILY.
MORE ABOUT HER IN A MINUTE.

I AM AN ONLY CHILD,

THOUGH I AM LUCKY TO HAVE SOME PRETTY COOL PARENTS.

DAD
· BRINGS ME COLORING BOOKS WHEN I'M SICK
· TELLS LOTS OF JOKES – SOME ARE FUNNY
MOM
· HELPS ME WITH MY HOMEWORK
· REALLY GREAT AT COMPUTERS AND MATH
ME

AND I AM REALLY HAPPY TO HAVE A DOG AND A CAT.

WE NAMED OUR DOG "TREAT" BECAUSE THAT'S THE ONLY WAY HE'LL COME WHEN WE CALL HIM.

WE NAMED OUR CAT "CAT" BECAUSE SHE WON'T COME NO MATTER WHAT WE SAY.

TREAT?

TRY TUNA.

I AM MANY THINGS, BUT ONE THING I AM NOT...

...IS "ENOUGH."

enough

\i'nəf\

ADJECTIVE

1. FILL A NEED. SUIT A PURPOSE. FIT THE BILL.

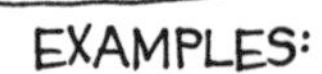

ATHLETIC ENOUGH

COOL ENOUGH

TALENTED ENOUGH

THEN THERE'S ME:

NOT ATHLETIC ENOUGH

NOT TALENTED ENOUGH

NOT COOL ENOUGH

SEE ALSO: NERDY, CLUMSY, AWKWARD.

"ENOUGH" IS ONE OF THOSE WORDS THAT LOOKS LIKE IT'S SPELLED WRONG EVEN WHEN IT ISN'T.

WHATEVER IT IS, I DON'T HAVE IT.

ENOUGH FRIENDS
(ESPECIALLY THE POPULAR ONES)

ENOUGH SUCCESS

ENOUGH STYLE

ENOUGH TALENT

EVEN IF IT CAME IN A JAR,
I WOULDN'T HAVE ENOUGH OF IT.

BUT AT LEAST I HAVE LILY.

WE'RE TWO PEAS IN A POD.

AND WE'VE BEEN BEST FRIENDS SINCE SECOND GRADE.

WE DO EVERYTHING TOGETHER. WE EVEN HAVE A CLUB.

EVERYTHING IN THE CLUB IS PURPLE BECAUSE THAT'S LILY'S FAVORITE COLOR. (I LIKE PINK.)

CLUB SOCKS

CLUB T-SHIRT

LILY LOVES TO SING, AND I GO TO CHORUS WITH HER. I CAN'T SING, SO I JUST STAND IN THE BACK AND PRETEND I'M SINGING.

A LOT OF KIDS DO THIS. IF IT WASN'T FOR THE FRONT ROW, WE WOULDN'T MAKE A SOUND.

OVER THE SUMMER, LILY MOVED TO ANOTHER PART OF TOWN.

EVER SINCE THEN SHE'S BEEN REALLY BUSY.

WHATCHA DOING?

I'M BUSY.

HOW 'BOUT NOW?

STILL BUSY.

AND AFTER THAT?

I'LL BE EVEN BUSIER.

I CAN'T WAIT FOR THE FIRST DAY OF MIDDLE SCHOOL TOMORROW, BUT IT WILL BE WEIRD GOING TO A MUCH LARGER SCHOOL WITH KIDS FROM ALL OVER TOWN.

I'M SO EXCITED LILY AND I HAVE LOCKERS NEXT TO EACH OTHER!

HOPEFULLY WE'LL BE IN THE SAME HOMEROOM!

NO MATTER WHAT, WE CAN EAT LUNCH TOGETHER!

I'M SO HAPPY TO HAVE MY BEST FRIEND TO SHARE THIS ADVENTURE WITH!

CHAPTER 1
MAGAZINE GiRL

THE NEXT MORNING I GOT READY FOR SCHOOL...

LILY AND I USUALLY WEAR THE SAME OUTFIT ON THE FIRST DAY. I TEXTED HER...

...BUT SHE'S NOT RESPONDING.

I REALLY DON'T HAVE ANYTHING TO WEAR.
HI!

MIRROR, MIRROR, ON THE WALL, WHO'S THE DORKIEST OF THEM ALL?
DON'T PUT ME ON THE SPOT.

FIRST-DAY-OF-SCHOOL PICTURES ARE THE WORST.

SO ARE FIRST-THING-CHRISTMAS-MORNING PICTURES.
MY MOM DOESN'T LIKE THOSE, EITHER.

I HOPPED ON MY BIKE, EXCITED TO GET TO SCHOOL AND SEE LILY.

THEY'RE WEARING THE SAME OUTFIT?

WHY ISN'T LILY WAITING UP FOR ME?

AM I LOSING MY BEST FRIEND?

MAGAZINE GiRL

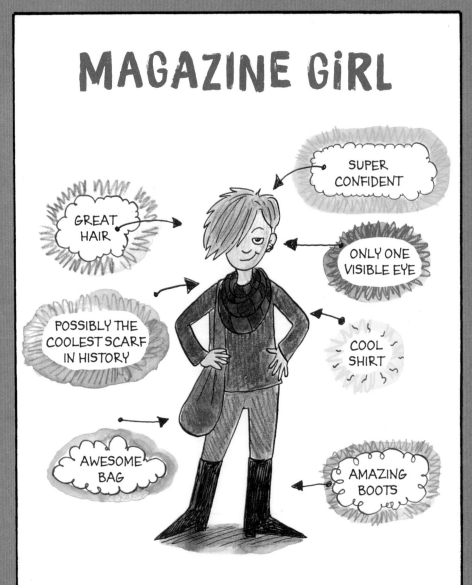

MAGAZINE GIRL HAS HAIR COVERING ONE EYE.
PEOPLE ARE MYSTERIOUS WHEN THEY COVER ONE EYE.

MAGAZINES ARE FUNNY. THEY'RE ALWAYS TELLING PEOPLE HOW TO LOOK AND WHAT TO WEAR AND THINGS THEY SHOULD BE DOING.

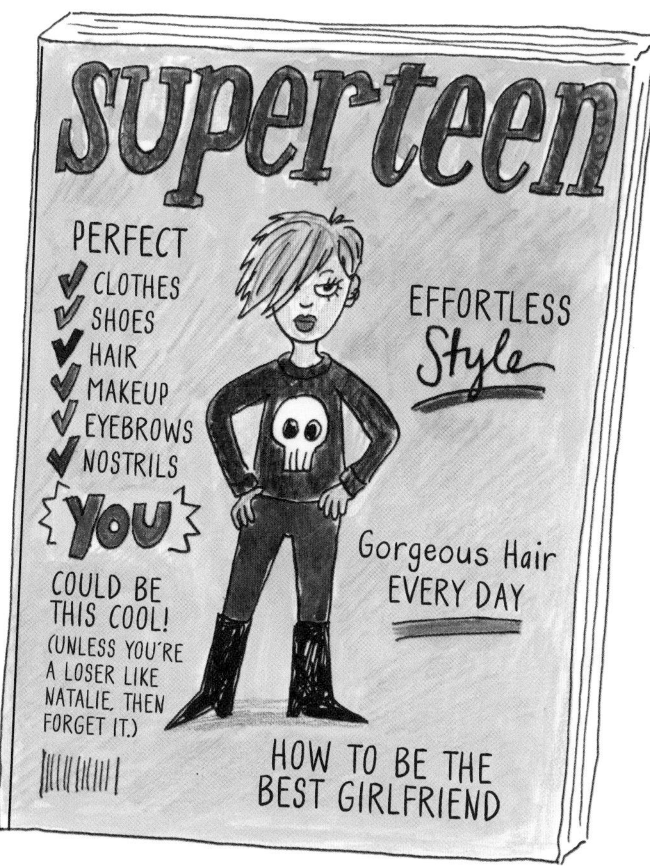

MAGAZINES TELL ME THAT MY CLOTHES AREN'T COOL ENOUGH, MY TEETH AREN'T WHITE ENOUGH, MY HAIR ISN'T EDGY ENOUGH, AND MY NOSTRILS AREN'T CUTE ENOUGH. ALSO, I HAVE TOO MANY PORES. (DON'T WE NEED PORES FOR SOMETHING?)

WHAT IF I FORGET THE COMBINATION?

HEY, LILY! AREN'T YOU HAPPY THAT WE'RE LOCKER NEIGHBORS?
WHATEVER.

WHAT'S WITH LILY?
WHY IS SHE IGNORING ME?
WHAT DID I DO WRONG?
I FEEL AWFUL.
I THOUGHT WE WERE BEST FRIENDS.
SEE YOU AT GYM?
DOES THIS HAVE SOMETHING TO DO WITH THAT OTHER GIRL?

CHAPTER 2
HURDLES AND OTHER OBSTACLES

DOG EXERCISES

CAT EXERCISES

I HAD TO GO TO GYM CLASS, THE WORST THING EVER.

I THOUGHT I COULD AVOID RUNNING IF I TIED MY SHOE FOR FIFTEEN MINUTES, BUT I ONLY ENDED UP MISSING THE WARM-UP.
TIE TIE TIE

TWO THINGS HAPPENED IN GYM CLASS.
ONE, I SAW THE CUTEST BOY I'D EVER SEEN.

AND TWO, LILY COMPLETELY IGNORED ME.

HEY, LILY!

I CAN'T BELIEVE SHE DIDN'T RUN THE WARM-UP.

YEAH, REALLY.

MAGAZINE GIRL IS A NATURAL ATHLETE.

I'VE GOT TO BUILD UP SPEED...

...LEAP AS HIGH AS I CAN...

...FLY THROUGH THE AIR EFFORTLESSLY AND...

CRASH! TUMBLE! WHAMMO! OUCH!

ARE YOU OKAY?
YES.

I'D TELL YOU TO GET BACK ON THE HORSE, BUT GO SEE THE NURSE INSTEAD.

LILY DIDN'T EVEN ASK ME IF I'M OKAY.

DO YOU WANT SOME HELP?
THANKS.

I'M ZOE.
I'M NATALIE.

ARE YOU OKAY?

I THINK SO. EVERYTHING SEEMS TO BE WORKING.

I CAN WALK YOU TO THE NURSE JUST IN CASE.

THANKS!

NO PROBLEM. NOW I GET TO LEAVE GYM EARLY. IT'S THE WORST!

CHAPTER 3

SNOOZEFEST

TO DO
8 AM – WAKE UP
9 AM – EAT
10 AM – MORNING NAP
11 AM – REST
12 PM – SIESTA
1 PM – RELAX
2 PM – SNOOZE
3 PM – AFTERNOON NAP
4 PM – EAT
5 PM – SLEEP

ZOE IS FROM ONE OF THE TWO OTHER ELEMENTARY SCHOOLS THAT FUNNELED INTO MIDWAY MIDDLE SCHOOL.
VERY SMART
BEST CURLS EVER
GREAT SMILE
REALLY NICE
KIND OF SHY
ALSO HATES GYM CLASS
SUPER HELPFUL
LOVES PEANUT BUTTER AND FLUFF SANDWICHES AS MUCH AS I DO
LOVES TO READ
PEANUT BUTTER
fluff
THE CRICKET IN TIMES SQUARE
(ORGANIC)
(NOT ORGANIC)

FEEL BETTER?
MUCH!
FIND YOUR VOICE STORY CONTEST! SEE MRS. GISBORNE FOR DETAILS
DO YOU SCUBA?
THANKS AGAIN! 
I'LL LOOK FOR YOU AT LUNCH!

AND WITH A FLIP OF HER HAIR, SHE WAS GONE.

* FOR YOUR EYES ONLY

I'M SO NERVOUS, AND MR. KELLY'S LECTURE ISN'T HELPING.

HE WON'T STOP TALKING ABOUT HIS PRIZE MUSKMELON.

THE ENTIRE CLASS WAS SNOOZING.
Z
M
HE WAS SMART TO BRING A TRAVEL PILLOW

THAT GIRL HAD SO MUCH HAIR IN HER FACE I COULDN'T TELL IF SHE'S ASLEEP OR NOT.
Z
ZZZZZZ

EVEN THE CLASS MOUSE WAS FAST ASLEEP.
Z

I THOUGHT I COULD SNEAK A PEEK AT THE NOTE UNDER THE DESK.

F.Y.E.O

CRINKLE CRINKLE
CRINKLE
Dear Natalie,
How are you? I am fine.
Now that we're in middle
school, I need to hang
with cooler people and you
not one of them. Maybe
If you gave me presents
every day I'd reconsider.
But probably not.

Dear Natalie,
How are you? I am fine.
Now that we're in middle school, I need to hang out with cooler people and you're not one of them. Maybe if you gave me presents every day I'd reconsider. But probably not.

Have a nice life,
LILY

P.S. I'll let you know if I need help with my homework.

I DON'T KNOW WHAT'S WORSE: GETTING DUMPED BY LILY OR TOTAL HUMILIATION.

SUDDENLY EVERYONE WAS WIDE AWAKE.

EXCEPT MAYBE THE GIRL WITH THE HAIR IN HER FACE.

AHEM
DEAR NATALIE,

HOW ARE YOU?

I AM FINE...

BRRING!

PHEW!

OKAY CLASS, THAT'S IT FOR TODAY. WE HAVE A VERY SPECIAL PROJECT COMING UP IN A FEW WEEKS!
AMPHIBIANS

WHY DOESN'T LILY LIKE ME ANYMORE?
FIND YOUR VOICE STORY CONTEST
SEE MRS. GISBORNE FOR DETAILS
IF SOMETHING DOESN'T ADD UP YOU MIGHT NEED A MATH TUTOR
DO YOU SCUBA?

I MET ZOE FOR LUNCH,
BUT I WASN'T HUNGRY.

WHAT WAS THAT
NOTE ABOUT?
SEE FOR
YOURSELF.

WHO'S
LILY?

SHE'S MY
BEST FRIEND.

SHE SOUNDS
LIKE A WORST
FRIEND.

I'D GIVE YOU
"FRENEMY"
AT BEST.

BUT WE'VE BEEN BEST FRIENDS SINCE SECOND GRADE.
WE USED TO DO EVERYTHING TOGETHER.
OUCH
HA HA!
SLAM
WE'D HAVE FUN ON THE SEESAW.
GRAPE SODA
GRAPE JELLY
GRAPE CANDY
WE HAD A CLUB TOGETHER. EVERYTHING WAS PURPLE.
LILY PICKED THE BEST HALLOWEEN COSTUMES.
EWWW, YOU'RE WEARING THAT?
SHE WAS ALSO MY FASHION CONSULTANT.

BUT EVER SINCE SHE MOVED, SHE'S BEEN SO BUSY.

SOUNDS LIKE SHE'S IGNORING YOU.

BUT SHE'S MY BEST FRIEND!

NOT ANYMORE.

THAT GIRL SHE'S WITH IS ALEX.

SHE'S KIND OF A LEGEND.

ALEX WAS THE MOST POPULAR GIRL IN MY ELEMENTARY SCHOOL.

SHE'S GOOD AT EVERYTHING.

SHE'S AN AMAZING ATHLETE, A GREAT SINGER...

SHE HAS THE COOLEST CLOTHES AND HAIR. SHE'S EVEN DONE SOME MODELING!

SHE ONLY HANGS OUT WITH THE MOST POPULAR KIDS.

ALEX CAN CHANGE YOUR ENTIRE SOCIAL STATUS JUST BY TALKING TO YOU!

YOUR "FRIEND" LILY MOVED INTO MY NEIGHBORHOOD THIS SUMMER.

I LIVE RIGHT NEAR ALEX.

WE ALL GO TO THE SAME POOL.

IT SOUNDS LIKE LILY IS TRYING TO MOVE UP THE FOOD CHAIN.

NO OFFENSE...

WERE YOU EVER FRIENDS WITH ALEX?

BACK IN FIRST GRADE, BUT I GUESS SHE DIDN'T THINK I WAS COOL ENOUGH, SO SHE STARTED IGNORING ME.

WHO'S THAT?

OH, THAT'S DEREK. HE WENT TO MY ELEMENTARY SCHOOL, TOO.

HE'S KINDA SHY, SO I DON'T KNOW HIM VERY WELL.

I KNOW HE'S REALLY SMART AND LIKES COMIC BOOKS.
TRAY

HE LIKES COMIC BOOKS?
YES, WHY?

NO REASON!
FIND YOUR VOICE STORY CONTEST SEE MRS GISBORNE FOR DETAILS
DO YOU SCUBA?

CHAPTER 4
RAINING CATS AND FROGS

THERE ARE PROBABLY WORSE THINGS THAN LOSING YOUR BEST FRIEND, BUT I CAN'T THINK OF ANY.

WORM SANDWICHES
(GROSS BUT NOT WORSE)

CHICKEN POX
(ITCHY BUT NOT WORSE)

ALIEN ABDUCTION
(WEIRD BUT NOT WORSE)

SARDINES
(EWW...STILL NOT WORSE)

HOMEWORK
(BUMMER BUT NOT WORSE)

QUICKSAND
(MESSY BUT NOT WORSE)

GIANT PYTHONS
(SCARY BUT NOT WORSE)

GETTING CHASED BY A GHOST
(CREEPY BUT NOT WORSE)

FAILED REPORT CARD
(BAD BUT NOT WORSE)

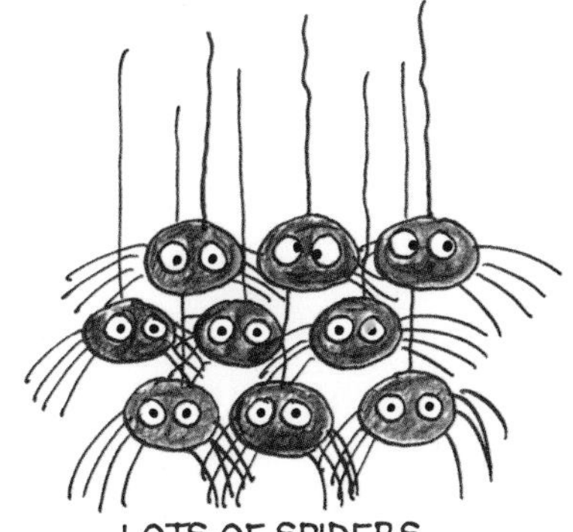

LOTS OF SPIDERS
(ALMOST WORSE)

THAT'S THE BEST
YOU COULD DO?

NATALIE
IS A
NERD

A FEW WEEKS LATER IN SCIENCE CLASS...

A VERY SMILEY GIRL SAT NEXT TO ME. TOO SMILEY.

WE LOVE
SCIENCE!
OKAY CLASS, TODAY WE WILL BE DISSECTING FROGS.

AND YOUR NEIGHBOR IS YOUR LAB PARTNER!

HI! I'M MILLIE! I'M VERY GOOD AT SCIENCE AND SCHOOL IN GENERAL.
I'M NATALIE.

NICE TO MEET YOU, NELLIE!
IT'S NATALIE.

WHATEVER YOU SAY, NAOMI.

I HAVE A VERY WEAK STOMACH AND AM ALLERGIC TO MOST AMPHIBIANS. ALSO, MY MOM SAID I DON'T HAVE TO DO ANYTHING I DON'T WANT TO DO, SO IT LOOKS LIKE YOU'RE GOING TO BE DOING MOST OF THE WORK. HAVE I MENTIONED THAT I'M GOOD AT EVERYTHING? YOU NAME IT, AND I'M GREAT AT IT. ASK ANYONE AND THEY'LL TELL YOU HOW GREAT I AM, IN CASE YOU CAN'T TELL ALREADY, BUT I KNOW YOU CAN.

HERE'S YOUR FROG.
EWW!

PRETTY MUCH THE LAST THING I WANT TO HEAR TODAY IS "HERE'S YOUR FROG."

DON'T WORRY, IT'S A SIMULATED FROG. THEY'RE MADE OUT OF JELL-O.

THESE FROGS DON'T HAVE MUCH OF A LIFE.
POKE
JIGGLE

SOUNDS FAMILIAR.

MY MOM WAS PRETTY UPSET ABOUT US DISSECTING REAL FROGS, SO SHE MADE THEM OUT OF JELL-O. BUT THERE WAS ONE PROBLEM...

LIME
ORANGE
STRAWBERRY-BANANA
CHERRY
LEMON
TROPICAL FUSION
PEACH
RASPBERRY
WATERMELON
THE STORE RAN OUT OF LIME JELL-O, SO MY MOM HAD TO MAKE THEM ALL OUT OF DIFFERENT FLAVORS, WHICH WAS WEIRD, BUT AT LEAST THEY SMELLED PRETTY GOOD.

I WAS TOO BUSY DOODLING TO EVEN THINK ABOUT CUTTING INTO THE FROG, EVEN IF IT WAS MADE OUT OF JELL-O.

THIS FROG HAS MORE OF A SOCIAL LIFE THAN I DO.

IT'S BAD ENOUGH THAT I'M BEING PUBLICLY HUMILIATED BY LILY, AND NOW I HAVE MILLIE FLATBOTTOM AS A LAB PARTNER.
STUCK UP (LIKE FLYPAPER)
BOSSY
PHONY (NOT THAT PHONE)
FAKE SMILE
ALWAYS FORGETS MY NAME
(NELLIE)
(NAOMI)
(NANCY)
(NINCOMPOOP)
THINKS SHE'S BETTER THAN EVERYONE ELSE
SHE'S NOT A CHEERLEADER, SHE JUST LIKES THE "M" FOR "MILLIE"
AND "ME"
OVERLY DRAMATIC
EATS THE CREAM OUT OF OREOS AND PUTS THE COOKIE BACK TOGETHER

ARE YOU GOING TO DO THIS OR WHAT?
POKE
POKE
JIGGLE
JIGGLE

I THINK THIS ONE IS STRAWBERRY-BANANA...
SNIFF

YOU'RE THE WORST LAB PARTNER EVER!

I SHOULD HAVE YOU FIRED!

I DESERVE BETTER THAN THIS!

SPLAT!

A LIME FROG HIT MILLIE IN THE FACE...

...AND CHAOS BROKE OUT, LEAVING JUICY, SQUISHY, FRUIT-FLAVORED JELL-O FROGS EVERYWHERE.

THAT'S ENOUGH! EXPERIMENT OVER!

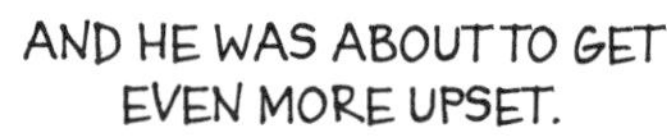

THE GIRL WITH HAIR IN HER FACE ACCIDENTALLY CUT INTO HIS PRIZE MUSKMELON.

HEART

FROG

LUNGS

VEINS

I THINK I FOUND THE GUTS!

BUT MR. KELLY WAS RIGHT ABOUT SOMETHING...

MUSKMELONS ARE DELICIOUS!

LILY CONTINUED TO IGNORE ME.

THAT WAS CRAZY ABOUT THE FROGS, HUH?

DID YOU HEAR SOMETHING?

SLAM

NOPE. NOTHING.

HA! WHAT A LOSER!

WHY WERE YOU EVEN FRIENDS WITH HER?

I AM SO LONELY WITOUT LILY.

LATER IN ENGLISH CLASS, ZOE COULD TELL I WAS UPSET.

WHAT'S GOING ON?
LILY'S IGNORING ME.

IGNORE HER BACK.
BUT SHE'S MY BEST FRIEND.

I THINK YOU NEED TO LOOK UP "FRIEND" IN THE DICTIONARY.

I KNOW ZOE MEANS WELL.

BUT I STILL WANT LILY BACK.

MRS. GISBORNE, OUR ENGLISH TEACHER, MADE AN ANNOUNCEMENT AT THE END OF CLASS...
I BEFORE E EXCEPT AFTER C (EXCEPT FOR THE EXCEPTIONS)
THERE IS A STATEWIDE STORY CONTEST, AND I ENCOURAGE ANYONE WHO IS INTERESTED TO ENTER!
FIND YOUR VOICE STORY CONTEST
I ♥ COFFEE

I CAN'T KEEP DOING NERDY THINGS IF I WANT TO GET LILY BACK.

NATALIE IS A LOSER!

JUST WHEN I THOUGHT THINGS COULDN'T GET ANY WORSE...

HI.

HI, I'M NATALIE.

ANYBODY EVER TELL YOU YOU'RE A DOG?

NATALIE IS
A DOGGGG!
NATALIE IS
A DOGGGG!

WOOF
WOOF
WOOF

HA HA HA!
WOOF! WOOF!
WOOF!

AND THAT'S HOW I MET SHAWN DREARY,
WHO WOULD BARK AT ME ANY CHANCE HE'D GET.

BEEP! BEEP!

C'MON BOOPSIE, LET'S GO!

RATS, THAT'S MY MOM.

BOOPSIE

BOOPSIE?

SHAWN'S RIGHT! I AM A DOG! AND A LOSER! NO WONDER LILY DOESN'T WANT TO BE FRIENDS WITH ME!

WHAT'S WRONG WITH BEING A DOG?

YOU'RE A BIGGER BULLY TO YOURSELF THAN ANY OF THOSE PEOPLE.

PLENTY.

WOOF!
NOT THAT I CAN BLAME YOU.

I HAVE TO FIGURE OUT HOW TO GET LILY BACK.

DACHSHUND GROWTH CHART

CHAPTER 5
HATS OFF

OPERATION: GET LILY BACK

STEP 1: LOOK COOLER

GET COOLER GLASSES

GET COOLER HAIR

GET COOLER BAG

GET COOLER CLOTHES

ACT COOLER OVERALL

GET COOLER SHOES

OPERATION: GET LILY BACK

STEP 2: DO COOLER THINGS

OPERATION: GET LILY BACK

STEP 3: HANG OUT WITH COOLER PEOPLE

OPERATION: GET LILY BACK

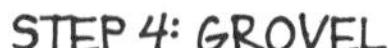

I STARTED "OPERATION GET LILY BACK" BY TRYING TO LOOK COOLER. THE MODEL ON THE COVER OF MY MOM'S MAGAZINE HAD A REALLY COOL HAT. I WAS SURE IF I HAD A HAT LIKE THAT, I'D LOOK COOL, TOO.

Glamorous
Fall Fashion issue
Wear Hats, BE COOL!
222 Hot New Looks!

I BEGGED MY MOM FOR AN ADVANCE ON MY BIRTHDAY PRESENT.

SHE AGREED, AND WE WENT TO THE MALL SO I COULD FIND THE PERFECT HAT.

I TRIED ON ALL KINDS OF HATS.

YOU CAN'T GET ANY MORE GLAMOROUS THAN THIS!

THANKFULLY, I ONLY HAVE TO WEAR THIS FOR A DAY.

BOUNCE
BOUNCE
BOUNCE

BOUNCE
BOUNCE

SWISH!
GRRRR

THE NEXT DAY AT SCHOOL, I WAITED BY MY LOCKER IN MY NEW HAT FOR LILY TO SHOW UP.

THAT WAS NOT THE REACTION
I WAS LOOKING FOR.

STUPID
HAT.

SO MUCH
FOR THAT.
SLAM

CHAPTER 6
CUPID STRIKES AGAIN

I HAD A HARD TIME LOOKING COOL IN MATH CLASS WHEN MR. SAKE CALLED ME TO LEAVE CLASS EARLY.

$\pi = 3.14$ OR

$E = mc^2$

$(a+b)^2 = a^2 + 2ab + b^2$

ALL ALP* STUDENTS, IT'S TIME TO GO!

IF THINGS DON'T ADD UP + YOU MIGHT NEED A MATH TUTOR

*ADVANCED LEARNING PROGRAM

A FEW OTHER STUDENTS LEAVE, TOO.

I'M SO EXCITED TO SEE DEREK LEAVE FOR ALP, TOO.

MAYBE NOW I'LL HAVE A CHANCE TO TALK TO HIM.

WHAT'S UP, DEREK?
TAP
TAP
TAP
TAP
WHO'S YOUR FAVORITE SUPERHERO?
TAP
TAP
TAP
TAP
SO...DID YOU GET THE MATH HOMEWORK?
TAP
TAP
TAP
TAP

TAP
TAP
TAP
TAP

WHAT CAN I SAY TO HIM? I HAVE TO THINK OF SOMETHING BEFORE THE BELL...
TAP
TAP
TAP
TAP

RINGS.
BRRRRINGGG!!!

THE MORE I GET TO KNOW DEREK, THE BIGGER MY CRUSH GETS...
SUPER CUTE
CUTEST SMILE EVER
FLIRT-CANCELING HEADPHONES
SWAMP THING
LOVES COMIC BOOKS
REALLY SMART
NATALIE + DEREK
N + M
D S
DEREK + NATALIE
ONLY EATS GRAPES IF THEY'RE PEELED
DEREK
LISTENS TO COOL MUSIC

ZOE WAITED FOR ME AFTER CLASS.

I HAVE THE BEST IDEA!

WHY DON'T YOU COME TO BALLROOM DANCING WITH ME?

LILY AND ALEX WILL BE THERE. AND DEREK.

DEREK?? I MEAN, DEREK? SO...?

IT'S SO OBVIOUS YOU LIKE HIM! IT'S WRITTEN ALL OVER YOUR FACE.

IT IS?

I
LIKE
DEREK

I WASN'T SURE ABOUT BALLROOM DANCING. BUT IF LILY WILL BE THERE, IT MUST BE COOL. MAYBE IT WILL MAKE ME COOLER TO BE THERE, TOO.

I WONDER IF I'LL FIT IN.

NOT IN THAT DRESS, TOOTS.

SWIPE

CHAPTER 7
DANCE
(BUT EVERYONE IS WATCHING)

THERE'S LILY AND ALEX AND DEREK!

I FEEL LIKE SOMEONE IS GOING TO ASK ME TO LEAVE.

THIS IS MY CHANCE TO TALK TO LILY...

I HOPE I DON'T SAY ANYTHING STUPID.

AND THEN SHE TOLD ME–
HEY, LILY, ISN'T THIS PLACE COOL?! CAN YOU BELIEVE HOW BIG THE COLUMNS ARE?
GO AWAY, NATALIE. NO ONE IS TALKING TO YOU.

SUDDENLY I FELT VERY SMALL.

ALL THE KIDS HAD TO LINE UP ON EITHER SIDE OF THE ROOM TO BE MATCHED UP WITH A PARTNER. I STOOD RIGHT ACROSS FROM DEREK.

IT'S AMAZING HOW EVERYONE ELSE IN THE ROOM DISAPPEARS...

THE INSTRUCTOR KNEW WE'D STAND NEAR THE PARTNER WE WANTED, SO SHE SAID:
YOUR PARTNER IS THE PERSON DIAGONAL FROM YOU!

I HAD A BAD FEELING ABOUT THIS. I WAS AFRAID TO LOOK...

IT WAS WORSE THAN I THOUGHT. IT WAS HIM. SHAWN DREARY!

EEK!

IN THIS LESSON, YOU ARE GOING TO DANCE WITH A BALLOON BETWEEN YOUR HEADS.

THIS WILL HELP WITH YOUR POISE AND POSTURE.

I DON'T KNOW WHICH WAS WORSE: GETTING IGNORED BY LILY OR HAVING TO DANCE WITH SHAWN. I THINK IT'S A TIE.

THE GIRL WITH HAIR IN HER FACE ENDED UP DANCING WITH A COATRACK.

YOU REALLY NEED TO LOOSEN UP.

BALLROOM DANCING WASN'T FUN... FOR ANYONE. AND I'M PRETTY SURE I DIDN'T GET ANY CLOSER TO GETTING LILY BACK.

CHAPTER 8
SING LIKE NO ONE CAN HEAR YOU

AUDITIONS TODAY! SCHOOL PLAY!
I CAN'T WAIT FOR THE SCHOOL PLAY TRYOUTS!
I HOPE I GET THE LEAD.
C'MON, LET'S GO.

MAYBE IF LILY AND I ARE IN THE PLAY TOGETHER WE'LL BE FRIENDS AGAIN.
AUDITIONS TODAY! SCHOOL PLAY!

AT LEAST IT'S NOT SINGING!

AUDITIONS TODAY! SCHOOL PLAY!

AUDITIONS TODAY!
SHOW TUNE MEDLEY!

AUDITIONS TODAY!
SHOW TUNE MEDLEY!

THANK YOU FOR COMING TO THE AUDITION!

THIS YEAR, INSTEAD OF A PLAY, WE ARE HAVING A SHOW TUNE MEDLEY!

WHAT??

EVERYONE WILL HAVE A CHANCE TO TRY OUT, BUT WE ONLY HAVE A FEW LEADS.

EVERYONE ELSE WILL PARTICIPATE AS BACKUP DANCERS, WHICH ARE STILL VERY IMPORTANT.

MY LIFE IS A GIANT PARTICIPATION AWARD.

ALEX WENT FIRST AND COMPLETELY NAILED IT.

LILY WAS SO GOOD SHE GOT A STANDING OVATION, AND SOMEONE THREW FLOWERS ONSTAGE DURING HER AUDITION!

THE GIRL WITH HAIR IN HER FACE COULDN'T FIND THE MICROPHONE AND SANG INTO A MOP.

THE ONLY SONG I KNOW ALL THE WORDS TO IS "HAPPY BIRTHDAY," BUT I USUALLY SING IT WITH A WHOLE GROUP OF PEOPLE AND CAN GET AWAY WITH MOUTHING THE WORDS LIKE I DO IN CHORUS.

HAPPY...

HAPPY BIRTHDAY TO YOOOOU...HAPPYYY BIRTHDAY TO YOOOOU... HAPPYY BIRTHDAY TO...UH...TO...

WAIT, WHO'S BIRTHDAY IS IT? UH...

UH...SANTA CLAUS, HAPPYYY BIRTHDAY TO YOOOOOOOOOOU!!!

SANTA CLAUS?!?
WHY DID I SAY THAT?
DOES HE EVEN HAVE A BIRTHDAY?

FIRST THERE WERE CRICKETS...
CHIRP
CHIRP
CHIRP
CHIRP

AND THEN THE WHOLE ROOM BROKE OUT IN LAUGHTER. I DON'T KNOW WHICH WAS WORSE.
HA HA HA HA HA HA HA
HA HA
HA HA HA HA
HA HA
HA HA HA
HA HA HA HA
HA HA
BWAHAHAHAHA

ZOE STOOD UP AND CLAPPED FOR ME, BUT SHE WAS THE ONLY ONE.
CLAP
CLAP
CLAP

WELL, SO DID THE GIRL WITH HAIR IN HER FACE, BUT SHE CLAPPED FOR EVERYONE.
CLAP
CLAP
CLAP

I WANTED TO CRAWL INTO A HOLE.
THAT'LL WORK.

ZOE AND I GOT TO BE BACKUP DANCING ANIMALS.

THE GIRL WITH HAIR IN HER FACE GOT TO BE A TREE.

MRS. BELLEVILLE ASKED ME TO BE A PARROT.

CHAPTER 9
COSTUMES, PLEASE

I WAS SO EXCITED TO DESIGN MY PARROT COSTUME!

BLUE, RED, AND YELLOW FEATHERS SEWN ON TO A BLACK LEOTARD, HAT WITH DETACHABLE BEAK, ORANGE TIGHTS, AND SNEAKERS

I HELPED ZOE DESIGN HER PENGUIN COSTUME, TOO.

BLACK PANTS, BLACK SHIRT, WHITE BIB,
WHITE HAT, ORANGE BEAK, AND SNEAKERS

A FEW WEEKS LATER, ZOE CAME OVER AFTER SCHOOL TO WORK ON OUR COSTUMES.

THANKS, NATALIE, THIS IS AMAZING! I LOVE IT!

SNIP

ALL I NEED NOW ARE BLACK CLOTHES, A WHITE BIB, AND A WADDLE.

THANKS FOR HELPING ME WITH MY WINGS!
IT'S FUN!

HOW MANY FEATHERS ARE LEFT?
ABOUT 6 MILLION...

WHAT ARE YOU GOING TO DO FOR MAKEUP?

I HAVE JUST THE THING!

I FOUND THESE PAINT PENS IN THE GARAGE. THEY WILL BE PERFECT FOR MY FACE PAINT!

ARE YOU SURE YOU CAN USE THOSE ON YOUR FACE?

I CAN'T SEE WHY NOT!

DO YOU THINK LILY WILL LIKE MY COSTUME?

WHAT DO YOU CARE WHAT SHE THINKS?

WE'RE BEST FRIENDS...

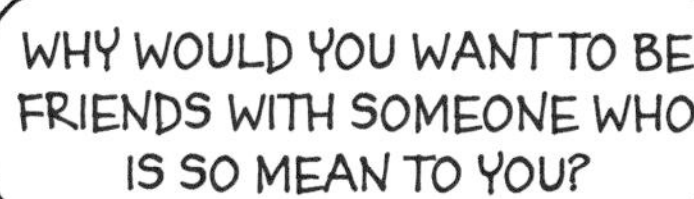
WHY WOULD YOU WANT TO BE FRIENDS WITH SOMEONE WHO IS SO MEAN TO YOU?

SHE WASN'T ALWAYS MEAN TO ME...

WELL, SHE IS NOW...

ZOE THINKS LILY IS MEAN TO ME.
C'MON, HONEY, HAS SHE EVER REALLY BEEN NICE TO YOU?
BEST CAT TOY EVER!
MY TAIL!

CHAPTER 10
SHOWSTOPPER

I'D BETTER BRING
SOME GLUE IN CASE
I LOSE A FEATHER.

AUDITORIUM

OH, NO! THE FLOWER BROKE OFF MY HEADBAND!

I BROUGHT GLUE!
GREAT!

HERE YOU GO!
UH... THANKS.

I GUESS THAT'S BIRDLIKE. MAYBE I SHOULD LOSE THE GLASSES.

MUCH MORE BIRDLIKE WITHOUT GLASSES.

WHAT ARE YOU DOING?
PRACTICING MY BIRD FACE...IT'S BETTER WITHOUT GLASSES.

COSTUMES, EVERYONE!

CAN YOU SEE OK WITHOUT YOUR GLASSES?
I THINK SO...

AHEM.
HUH? OH.

HEY, LILY! WHAT DO YOU THINK OF MY COSTUME?
WHAT ARE YOU SUPPOSED TO BE?
I'M A PARROT! 
YOU LOOK LIKE A DORK TO ME.

I'M NEEDED ONSTAGE.

LILY AND ALEX SANG THE OPENING SONG...

WHILE WE WAITED BACKSTAGE FOR OUR TURN.
M

SHAWN WAS DRESSED
AS A ROCK...

...AND INSISTED ON
SITTING BEHIND ME.

DEREK WAS AN ADORABLE
FROG, BUT HE DIDN'T THINK SO.

THIS IS SO
EMBARRASSING!

HOW AM I SUPPOSED
TO DANCE IN
FLIPPERS?
FLIP
FLOP
FLIP
FLOP

AND THE GIRL WITH HAIR IN HER FACE HAD A HARD TIME MOVING AROUND AS A TREE.

DO TREES EVEN DANCE?

WE WAITED FOR OUR CUE.

I GOT TO WALK BEHIND DEREK.

EVERYTHING WAS GOING PRETTY WELL UNTIL WE STARTED DANCING.

WE WERE ALL HAVING A GREAT TIME UNTIL...

SLAM

BWAHAHAHAHAHA!

HAHAHA!
I'M SO EMBARRASSED!
PLUCK!

ARE YOU KIDDING?

THAT WAS THE BEST THING TO HAPPEN IN THE ENTIRE SHOW!

AND WE TOOK THE SPOTLIGHT OFF ALEX AND LILY FOR A CHANGE.

THE SHOW MUST GO ON! GET UP!

I'D BETTER PUT MY GLASSES BACK ON!
PLUCK!

AND THAT'S HOW I MET "THE GIRL WITH HAIR IN HER FACE," ALSO KNOWN AS FLO.

LILY AND ALEX SANG THE ENCORE AND BOWED.
CLAP
CLAP
CLAP
CLAP
CLAP

THEY GOT A STANDING OVATION.

WE ALSO TOOK A BOW, AND THE AUDIENCE ROARED!
CLAP
CLAP
CLAP
CLAP
CLAP
CLAP

LILY AND ALEX GOT BOUQUETS OF FLOWERS...

AND I GOT A BOUQUET OF FEATHERS.

FIND YOUR VOICE STORY! CONTEST! SEE MRS. GISBORNE FOR DETAILS

!!!

HOPEFULLY IT WILL FADE BY TOMORROW.

WHAT IF IT
DOESN'T?

NATALIE HAS
A BIRD FACE!
NATALIE HAS
A BIRD FACE!

CHAPTER 11
SMOKE AND MIRRORS

MIRROR, MIRROR, ON THE WALL, WHO'S THE...
DON'T WORRY, YOU'RE PURRFECT!

THE NEXT MORNING...

THIS WILL COVER IT UP.

MAYBE NO ONE WILL NOTICE...

THANKS
FOR RUINING
THE PLAY,
DORK!

ARE YOU THAT COLD?

MY FACE PAINT DIDN'T COME OFF.
OH, THAT'S AWFUL!

I GUESS YOU'LL NEVER FORGET THIS SCHOOL PHOTO...

LILY AND ALEX LOOKED LIKE SUPERMODELS.

SHAWN LOOKED MEAN.

MILLIE WORE A TIARA.

Swoooooon

ZOE LOOKED CUTE.

DEREK LOOKED DREAMY!

FLO WORE HER TREE COSTUME BECAUSE SHE LIKED IT SO MUCH.

AND I LOOKED LIKE I ROBBED A SKI SLOPE.

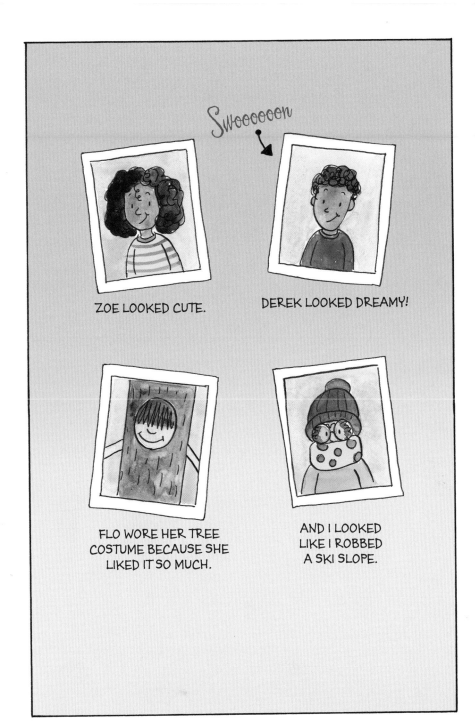

LATER AT LUNCH...
THIS IS JUST PERFECT.
WHAT DO YOU MEAN?

THAT CLASS PHOTO'S GOING TO SHOW EVERYONE HOW BIG OF A DORK I AM!

HEY, DON'T TALK ABOUT MY FRIEND THAT WAY!

IT'S JUST A LITTLE FACE PAINT.

IT MAKES YOU UNIQUE.

YOU LOOKED GREAT!

THANKS!

SO DID DEREK!

HAHA! I KNEW YOU LIKED HIM!

CAN I SIT WITH YOU?
SURE!

ARE YOU GUYS ENTERING THE STORY CONTEST?

IT'S TOO NERDY.

I DON'T NEED TO LOOK LIKE ANY MORE OF A LOSER THAN I AM.

WHY DO YOU CARE WHAT PEOPLE THINK?

I'M TRYING TO GET LILY BACK, AND SHE THINKS IT'S NERDY.

BUT LILY ISN'T EVEN NICE TO YOU.

BESIDES, YOU HAVE SOME PRETTY COOL FRIENDS RIGHT HERE!

WELL, THAT'S TRUE...!

MAYBE YOU SHOULD FOCUS ON WHO YOU ARE INSTEAD OF WHO YOU AREN'T.

WORKS FOR ME!

BRRING!

WE'D BETTER GET TO ENGLISH!

FIND YOUR VOICE
STORY CONTEST
SEE

CHAPTER 12
A DAY IN THE LIFE

TO DO
8 AM – EAT
9 AM – BARK AT SQUIRRELS
10 AM – BARK AT NOTHING
11 AM – NAP
12 PM – BARK AT THE CAT
1 PM – BEG FOR TREATS
2 PM – BARK AT A FLY
3 PM – NAP
4 PM – SLEEP
5 PM – EAT

NEXT WEEK WE'RE DOING A CREATIVE WRITING EXERCISE, AND IT MUST BE DONE IN CLASS.
FIND YOUR VOICE STORY CONTEST
SEE MRS. GISBORNE FOR DETAILS

THE TOPIC IS "A DAY IN THE LIFE."

IN THE MEANTIME, THINK ABOUT HOW YOU WILL EXPRESS YOURSELF... AN ESSAY, A SONG, A HAIKU...

BE CREATIVE!

I CAN'T WAIT TO SEE WHAT YOU COME UP WITH!

BUT ALL I COULD THINK ABOUT WAS HOW TO GET DEREK'S ATTENTION.

EVERY TIME I LOOK OVER AT HIM HE LOOKS AWAY.

HE LOOKS EMBARRASSED.

OH! MAYBE IT'S MY HAT!
OR, MY BIRD FACE.

OK, NOW I'M EMBARRASSED.

AND DON'T FORGET ABOUT THE STATEWIDE STORY CONTEST!

THE WINNER GETS TO SHARE THEIR WORK WITH THE ENTIRE SCHOOL!

AND GETS A SPECIAL TRIP TO THE STATE CAPITAL!

I THOUGHT ABOUT WHAT FLO SAID AT LUNCH.
MAYBE YOU SHOULD FOCUS ON WHO YOU ARE INSTEAD OF WHO YOU AREN'T.

I'VE SPENT SO MUCH TIME THINKING ABOUT WHAT I'M NOT GOOD AT...

...THAT I NEVER THINK ABOUT WHAT I **AM** GOOD AT...
ACTUAL FROG
JELL-O FROG
NO SOCIAL LIFE

WAIT! THERE IS SOMETHING I'M GOOD AT. I'LL DRAW THE CREATIVE WRITING EXERCISE!
ACTUAL FROG
JELL-O FROG

CHAPTER 13
ABOUT TIME

I GOT TO CLASS REALLY EARLY.

I DIDN'T HAVE MUCH TIME, SO I WANTED TO BE SURE MY DESK WAS ALL SET UP.

HELLO, CLASS, I'M MR. DRIBBLE, YOUR SUBSTITUTE TEACHER.
SUB
#1 SUB

MRS. GISBORNE IS OUT SICK, SO I WILL LEAD THE IN-CLASS ASSIGNMENT.
SUB

YOU HAVE EXACTLY ONE HOUR...

GOOD LUCK!
SUB

READY...

SET...

GO!

I HAVE TO WORK REALLY QUICKLY.

AND I'M SO EXCITED ABOUT THE TOPIC.

I'M DRAWING "A DAY IN THE LIFE OF A FROG IF SHE WASN'T MADE OUT OF JELL-O."

12
1
2
3
4
5
6
7
8
9
10
11

I ALREADY HAD SKETCHES OF THE FROG FROM SCIENCE CLASS.
JELL-O FROG
ACTUAL FROG

IT'S SO MUCH FUN MAKING UP A STORY ABOUT HER.

YIKES! ONLY 30 MINUTES LEFT! I'M NOT EVEN HALFWAY DONE!

WHAT IF I DON'T FINISH IN TIME?

YOU GOT THIS!

SUB

WOW, MR. DRIBBLE FELL ASLEEP!

NO WONDER HIS NAME IS MR. DRIBBLE.

NOW I JUST HAVE TO COLOR IT IN...

POW!
SPLASH!

TWO MINUTES!

ONE MINUTE!

I STILL HAVE TO SIGN IT!

PENCILS DOWN!
NAT

OKAY, CLASS, PUT YOUR FINISHED WORK HERE ON THE DESK ON YOUR WAY OUT.
SUB

MRS. GISBORNE WILL REVIEW THEM WHEN SHE RETURNS TOMORROW.
SUB

SUB

YAWN
WAIT, YOU DREW THAT?
UH, YEAH.
SUB

WOW! THAT'S SO COOL!

AND AMAZING THAT YOU DID ALL OF THAT IN CLASS!

YOU'RE REALLY GOOD AT DRAWING!
THANKS!

I CAN'T EVEN DRAW A STICK FIGURE.

I THOUGHT ALEX WAS GOOD AT EVERYTHING.

I CAN'T BELIEVE THERE'S SOMETHING SHE'S NOT GOOD AT...

HOW'D IT GO?
&

IT WAS FUN! I CAN'T WAIT TO SHOW MRS. GISBORNE.
HOW 'BOUT YOU GUYS?

I WROTE A HAIKU ABOUT BELLY BUTTON LINT!

I WROTE ABOUT A GIRAFFE WHO LOVES FLOWERS.
I CAN'T WAIT TO HEAR WHAT YOU WROTE!

DID YOU GET IT ALL DONE?

ALMOST. I DIDN'T FINISH SIGNING MY NAME.

I ONLY GOT TO "NAT" WHEN MR. DRIBBLE YELLED PENCILS DOWN!

MAYBE THAT'S YOUR NEW PEN NAME!
GOOD IDEA!

YOU'RE REALLY GOOD AT DRAWING!

ALEX CAN CHANGE YOUR ENTIRE SOCIAL STATUS JUST BY TALKING TO YOU!

I COULDN'T WAIT TO GO TO SCHOOL THE NEXT DAY TO SHARE MY STORY WITH THE CLASS.

CHAPTER 14
WHAT'S THE STORY?

THE NEXT DAY AT SCHOOL...
HELLO, CLASS!

I'M SO EXCITED TO HEAR WHAT YOU CAME UP WITH!

ANY VOLUNTEERS WANT TO COME UP AND SHARE?

MEEE!
OKAY, FLO!

FLO, CAN YOU FACE THE CLASS?

AHEM. I WROTE A HAIKU ABOUT BELLY BUTTON LINT.

BELLY BUTTON LINT,
I SEE YOU IN MY NAVEL.
LIVING A SHORT LIFE.
THAT WAS A PERFECTLY 
FORMED HAIKU, FLO!

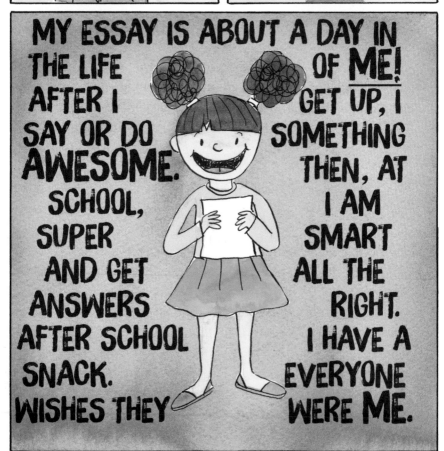

MY ESSAY IS ABOUT A DAY IN THE LIFE OF **ME!**

AFTER I GET UP, I SAY OR DO SOMETHING **AWESOME.**

THEN, AT SCHOOL, I AM SUPER SMART AND GET ALL THE ANSWERS RIGHT.

AFTER SCHOOL I HAVE A SNACK.

EVERYONE WISHES THEY WERE **ME.**

GULP!

FOR MY IN-CLASS ASSIGNMENT, I DREW A COMIC CALLED "A DAY IN THE LIFE OF A JELL-O FROG IF SHE WASN'T MADE OUT OF JELL-O."

NATALIE, CAN YOU
PLEASE PUT THOSE
ON THE TABLE SO WE
CAN ALL SEE?

THAT'S REALLY WONDERFUL, NATALIE.

BUT HOW DID YOU DO ALL THIS IN ONE HOUR?

UMM...

THE ASSIGNMENT WAS TO BE DONE DURING CLASS.

YOU COULDN'T HAVE FINISHED IT IN THAT AMOUNT OF TIME.

I'M SO SORRY, NATALIE...
BUT... BUT...

...IT'S NOT FAIR TO THE OTHER STUDENTS.
DON'T CRY. DON'T CRY.

BUT I DID.

MRS. GISBORNE?
YES, ALEX.

NATALIE DID DRAW HER COMIC IN CLASS.
I SAW HER.

ME TOO.
ME THREE.
UH-HUH.
I SAW HER.
YES, SHE DID!

EVEN SHAWN BACKED ME UP.
SHE DID.
WHEN SHE WASN'T SCRATCHING HER FLEAS.

IS THIS TRUE?
NOD
NOD

I'M SORRY I DOUBTED YOU.

YOU DESERVE AN A!

YAY!
HOORAY!
YES!
M

OKAY, CLASS, THAT'S ENOUGH FOR TODAY.
GREAT JOB, EVERYONE!

NATALIE, WILL YOU STAY AFTER CLASS FOR A MINUTE?
GULP

THIS COMIC WOULD BE GREAT FOR THE STORY CONTEST!

YOU ONLY NEED A FEW MORE PAGES...

AND I CAN HELP YOU PUT IT TOGETHER.

YOU NEED TO LET ME KNOW SOON. THE DEADLINE IS IN A FEW WEEKS!
I WILL!

SHOULD I ENTER THE BOOK CONTEST?
I LOVED WORKING ON THE COMIC.
I NEVER WIN ANYTHING.
WILL LILY THINK I'M A NERD?
DO I CARE?

CHAPTER 15
WHAT'S FOR LUNCH?

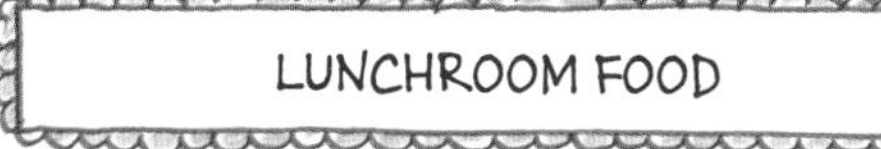

MYSTERY MEAT

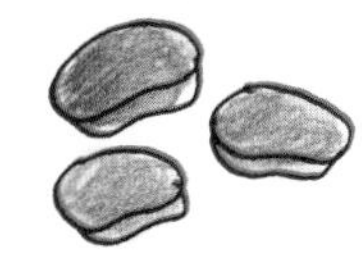

MYSTERY NUGGET

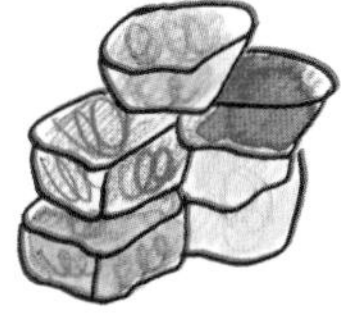

MYSTERY FRUIT

PIZZA

HEY,
NATALIE!

COME SIT
WITH US!

NERD
LOSER
GEEK
OUCH!
HAHA!
NO ONE IS TALKING TO YOU!
YOU'RE WEARING THAT??

OR...

WHY DO YOU CARE WHAT PEOPLE THINK?
WHY WOULD YOU WANT TO BE FRIENDS WITH SOMEONE WHO IS SO MEAN TO YOU?
FOCUS ON WHO YOU ARE.
YOU HAVE SOME PRETTY GREAT FRIENDS RIGHT HERE!

THANKS FOR ASKING, BUT...

...I'M SITTING WITH MY FRIENDS OVER THERE.

HI, GUYS!
HI!

WHAT DID MRS. GISBORNE SAY?

SHE THINKS I SHOULD ENTER THE STORY CONTEST.

AND?

I THINK I WILL!

AWESOME!

CHAPTER 16
THE ENVELOPE, PLEASE

I GOT TO WORK.
YOU
BE
YOU

HOW TO MAKE A BOOK:

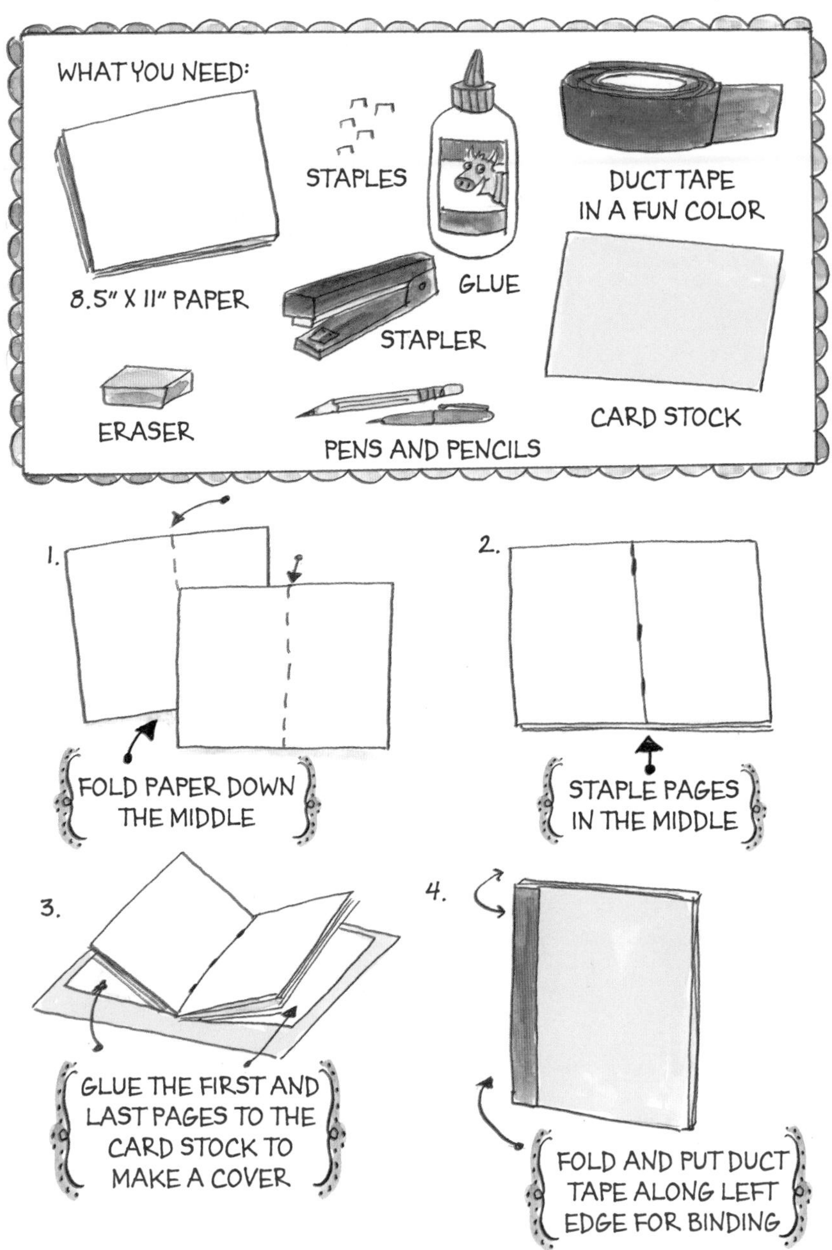
WHAT YOU NEED:
8.5" X 11" PAPER
STAPLES
GLUE
STAPLER
DUCT TAPE
IN A FUN COLOR
CARD STOCK
ERASER
PENS AND PENCILS
1.
FOLD PAPER DOWN
THE MIDDLE
2.
STAPLE PAGES
IN THE MIDDLE
3.
GLUE THE FIRST AND
LAST PAGES TO THE
CARD STOCK TO
MAKE A COVER
4.
FOLD AND PUT DUCT
TAPE ALONG LEFT
EDGE FOR BINDING

5. HAVE FUN WRITING AND DRAWING YOUR BOOK!

THEN MRS. GISBORNE HELPED ME MAIL MY BOOK INTO THE CONTEST. WE PUT IT IN A BIG ENVELOPE WITH CARDBOARD AND EXTRA STAMPS.

AND THEN I WAITED...
DON'T LET ANYONE DIM YOUR SPARKLE
DACHSHUND GROWTH
THIS TIME, I'M READY.

A FEW WEEKS PASSED...
HMM... NO NOTE!

I WAS FINALLY TALKING TO DEREK IN OUR ALP CLASS.
HEY, NATALIE! DO YOU, UH, WANT TO CHECK OUT THESE COMICS?

AND LAUGHING WITH ZOE AND FLO.

THE NEXT DAY IN ENGLISH CLASS...
GOOD MORNING! I HAVE A VERY SPECIAL ANNOUNCEMENT TO MAKE!

I HAVE THE RESULTS FOR THE STATEWIDE STORY CONTEST!

THIS IS IT!

YOU GOT THIS.

OH PLEASE, PLEASE, PLEASE NOT ANOTHER PARTICIPATION AWARD...

AND THE WINNER IS...

OUR VERY OWN...

NATALIE!

I CAN'T
BELIEVE IT!

WE KNEW YOU
COULD DO IT!

I WAS SO HAPPY I WAS SMILING
LIKE MILLIE FLATBOTTOM!

I WENT TO THE STATE CAPITAL FOR THE AWARDS CEREMONY.

WE GOT OUR AWARDS AND TOOK PICTURES.
EVEN THE GOVERNOR WAS THERE!

I DIDN'T MIND HAVING MY PICTURE TAKEN.
I DEFINITELY WANT A MEMORY OF TODAY!

MY FIRST PLACE TROPHY REALLY STOOD OUT IN MY SEA OF PARTICIPATION AWARDS.

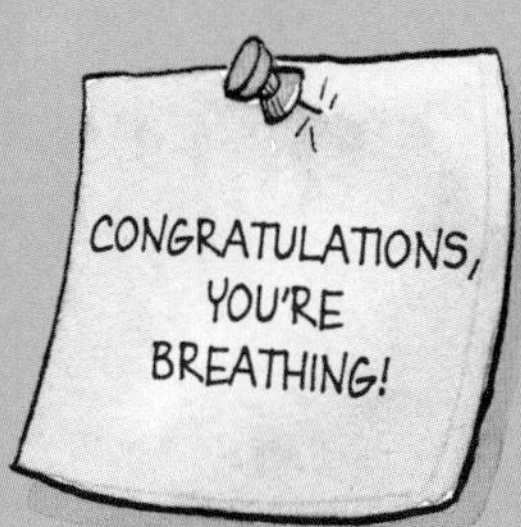

CHAPTER 17
STAND UP

THE NEXT DAY, MRS. GISBORNE ASKED ME TO PRESENT MY BOOK TO THE ENTIRE SIXTH GRADE. I WORE MY FAVORITE HAT.

EVERYONE WAS ASKING ME QUESTIONS...

WHERE DO YOU GET YOUR IDEAS?

THIS IDEA CAME FROM THE JELL-O FROG IN SCIENCE CLASS.

IDEAS ARE EVERYWHERE. WHEN I GET ONE I PUT IT IN MY SKETCHBOOK.

WHAT KIND OF PEN DO YOU USE?
M

I LIKE COLORED PENCILS AND MARKERS.

WHAT'S YOUR FAVORITE FLAVOR FROG?

IT'S A TOSS-UP BETWEEN LIME AND TROPICAL FUSION.

THAT WAS
REALLY COOL,
NATALIE!
M

MILLIE FLATBOTTOM
GOT MY NAME RIGHT!

YEAH COOL
BOOK,
NATALIE.
WHAT, ARE YOU
GOING TO BARK
AT ME, NOW?

NAH. DOGS CAN'T
WRITE COMICS.
THEY DON'T
HAVE THUMBS.

THAT WAS, LIKE,
REALLY COOL
AND STUFF.

AND I, UM,
WELL...
HEY,
NATALIE!

I'D BETTER GO...

DID I SOUND WEIRD UP THERE?
NO!

OKAY, GOOD!

AND EVEN IF YOU DID...

... I'M PRETTY SURE THE WEIRDEST PEOPLE HAVE THE MOST FUN.

UGH. I THOUGHT
LILY WAS OVER
IT ALREADY.
SIGH HERE 
WE GO AGAIN...

Dear Natalie,
How are you? I am fine.
Congratulations! I loved
your book and I loved
your bird costume. See
ya in class.
— Derek

WHAT DID
SHE SAY?

IT'S NOT
FROM LILY...

I'M SMILING LIKE
MILLIE FLATBOTTOM
AGAIN!

HE SAID
"LOVED."

TWICE!

I RACED ALL THE WAY HOME!

HE SAID "LOVED."
TWICE!

I THINK THINGS ARE LOOKING UP!
OKAY, I'M OUTTA HERE.

A DAY IN THE LIFE OF A FROG IF SHE WASN'T MADE OUT OF JELL-O
BY NATALIE MARIANO

STRAWBERRY–BANANA WAS A JELL–O FROG. SHE LIVED IN SCIENCE CLASS WITH THE OTHER JELL–O FROGS: LIME, LEMON, ORANGE, RASPBERRY, AND PEACH.

THE FROGS DIDN'T DO MUCH EXCEPT JIGGLE UNTIL ONE DAY...

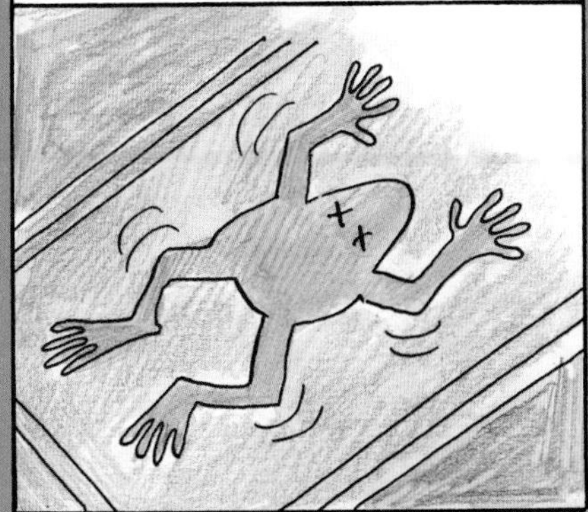

...THE SCIENCE TEACHER ADDED TOO MUCH MAGICAL GROWTH ELIXIR TO HIS MUSKMELON.

THERE WAS AN EXPLOSION! MUSKMELON AND MAGICAL ELIXIR SPLASHED ALL OVER THE FROGS!

POW!
SPLASH!
WHAMMO!

THEY ALL BECAME REAL FROGS!
NEAT!
COOL!
LEMON
LIME
SWEET!
AWESOME!
ORANGE
RASPBERRY
YIPEE!
YAY!
PEACH
STRAWBERRY–BANANA

THEY ALL HAD SPECIAL TALENTS. LIME COULD DANCE.

LEMON COULD SING.

AND PURPLE COULD JUMP REALLY HIGH.
WOW!
WHOA!
COOL!

BUT STRAWBERRY–BANANA COULDN'T DO ANY OF THOSE THINGS.
SIGH

SHE TRIED TO SING...
CROAK

SHE TRIED TO DANCE...
WHOOPS

AND SHE COULDN'T JUMP VERY FAR AT ALL.
SPLAT
BOUNCE

I CAN'T DO ANY OF THOSE THINGS.

STRAWBERRY–BANANA FELT SAD.
SNIFF

RASPBERRY AND PEACH HOPPED OVER FOR A VISIT.

WHY THE LONG FACE?

I CAN'T SING. I CAN'T DANCE. AND I CAN'T JUMP VERY FAR.

MAYBE YOU SHOULD FOCUS ON WHO YOU ARE INSTEAD OF WHO YOU AREN'T.

WORKS FOR ME!

HMM.

WHO AM I? WHAT CAN I DO?

SHE FOUND OUT SHE COULD RIDE A BIKE.

AND ICE SKATE BACKWARD.

TURNS OUT SHE COULD DO ALL KINDS OF THINGS!

AND SHE WAS HAVING SO MUCH FUN FIGURING OUT ALL THAT SHE COULD DO...

WHAT'S BLACK AND WHITE AND RED ALL OVER?

...THAT SHE DIDN'T WORRY ABOUT WHAT SHE COULDN'T DO.

AND MAYBE WITH SOME PRACTICE, SOMEDAY SHE COULD DO THOSE OTHER THINGS, TOO!

SPLAT

SLLIIIPP

MAYBE A LOT OF PRACTICE.

UNTIL THEN, SHE WAS HAPPY BEING HERSELF.

The End!

NAT

MARIA SCRIVAN is an award-winning cartoonist, illustrator, and author based in Stamford, Connecticut. Her laugh-out-loud syndicated comic, *Half Full*, appears daily in newspapers nationwide and on gocomics.com. Maria licenses her work for greeting cards throughout the United States and United Kingdom, and her cartoons have also appeared in *MAD Magazine*, *Parade*, and many other publications. Visit Maria online at mariascrivan.com.